THE REPUBLIC OF CEBU

A Blueprint for Creating a Micronation

Prof. Basilio Ojas, PhD.

BMN Publishing

Contents

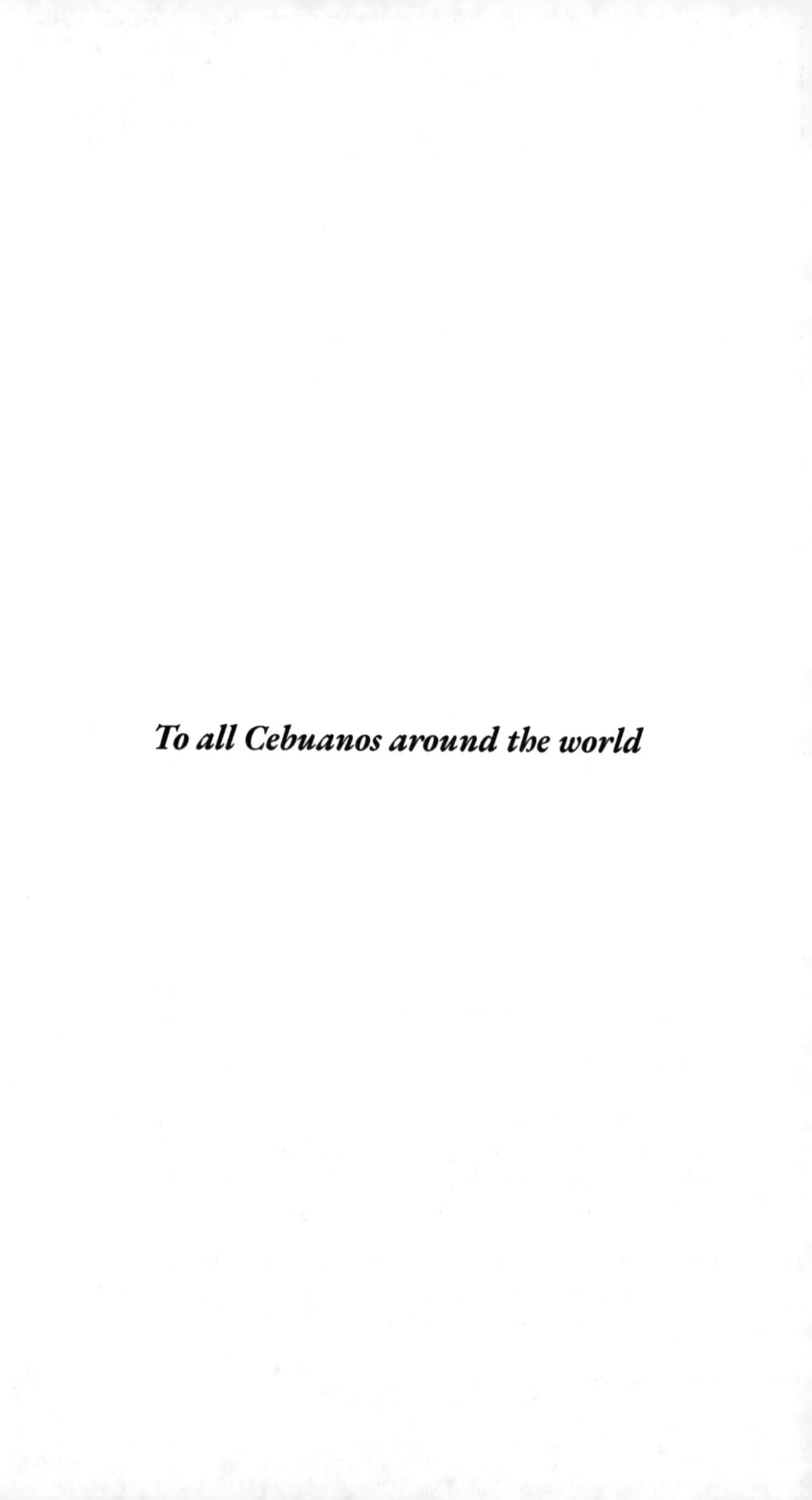

To all Cebuanos around the world

The Dream of Cebu as a Micronation

Throughout history, the idea of self-determination and autonomy has inspired countless individuals and regions around the world. Today, this desire to carve out a unique identity and establish independent governance is often pursued through the creation of micronations. Micronations are small, self-declared entities that claim independence from larger, recognized states, often for symbolic, artistic, or experimental reasons. Although most micronations are not legally recognized by other governments, they represent a fascinating exploration of sovereignty, identity, and governance.

The island of Cebu, a historically and culturally significant region of the Philippines, is an ideal candidate for a micronation. Rich in history, deeply rooted in its culture, and economically vibrant, Cebu could become a symbolic micronation that highlights its unique contributions to Filipino heritage while exploring concepts of autonomy and self-governance.

In an age of increasing globalization, local identities are often diluted or overlooked. Cebu, with its proud heritage—from the resistance of Lapu-Lapu to the vibrancy of the Sinulog Festival—deserves a platform that honors its individuality while embracing its role within the broader national and global community. A micronation offers a way for Cebuanos to celebrate their shared values, champion environmental sustainability, and cultivate a civic culture built on creativity, cooperation, and pride in place.

At its heart, the concept of Cebu as a micronation is not about separation, but elevation—a way to amplify the island's voice and agency in shaping its future. It invites citizens to participate more deeply in civic life, encourages cultural preservation, and sparks innovation in governance and community-building. By creating a symbolic nation rooted in history, culture, and vision, Cebu has the opportunity to serve as a model for how regions can assert their identity in empowering, peaceful, and imaginative ways.

In this book, we will explore the practical, legal, and creative steps required to establish Cebu as a micronation. We will examine historical precedents, the role of national identity, the legal challenges that come with such a project, and the symbolic importance of micronations in modern society.

Whether you're a history buff, a political theorist, or simply someone with an interest in building a creative community, this book offers a comprehensive blueprint for turning Cebu into a symbolic micronation that stands out on the global stage.

Chapter 1

Understanding Cebu's Identity & Historical Context

Cebu has long been one of the most important provinces in the Philippines. Its central location in the Visayas made it a crucial trading hub in precolonial times, with local leaders establishing connections with merchants from China, India, and Southeast Asia.

When Ferdinand Magellan arrived in Cebu in 1521, marking the beginning of Spanish colonial rule in the Philippines, it became the starting point of the nation's modern history.

For centuries, Cebu has maintained a strong sense of identity, both within the context of Spanish rule and as part of the independent Philippines.

Its role in Filipino nationalism, trade, and religion (as the cradle of Catholicism in the country) makes it uniquely positioned as a focal point for autonomy and self-expression.

Exploring these historical roots allows us to envision the transformation of Cebu into a symbolic micronation.

Cultural, Economic, and Geopolitical Importance of Cebu

We cannot overstate Cebu's economic contributions to the Philippines. As one of the most developed provinces in the country, it has a strong industrial base, tourism, and a robust service sector.

Cebu's economy would be one of the cornerstones of any future micronation project, as it already possesses the infrastructure needed for self-sufficiency.

Culturally, Cebu is also distinct. Millions of people across the Visayas and Mindanao speak Cebuano, the local language. The island's festivals, particularly the Sinulog Festival, are major cultural events that celebrate the region's unusual combination of indigenous, Spanish, and modern Filipino influences.

Historical Movements for Autonomy and Independence in the Region

Throughout Cebu's history, there have been movements, both symbolic and real, advocating for more autonomy or even independence. While no full-fledged independence movement has ever succeeded, the desire for more localized governance has been an undercurrent in Cebuano political thought.

This desire for self-determination dates back to the colonial period when local leaders pushed back against Spanish rule, most notably Lapu-Lapu's defiance during Magellan's arrival.

In modern times, Cebu has enjoyed a degree of autonomy through local governance under the framework of the Philippine Constitution. However, regional pride and a desire to differentiate Cebu's governance from that of the national government in Manila persist, with many Cebuanos feeling that Manila-based policies do not always reflect their needs.

This history of regional autonomy provides a rich foundation for the creation of a micronation, even if symbolic.

Why Cebu Could Be an Ideal Candidate for a Micronation

Cebu's strong economy, distinct culture, and historical significance make it an ideal candidate for a micronation. Geographic separation from Luzon, the Philippine government's seat, fosters a sense of regional identity that can manifest through self-governance.

Additionally, Cebu's history as a trading hub and its relatively independent political history within the context of the Philippines strengthen its candidacy.

A Cebuano micronation would not be about seceding from the Philippines in a formal sense but rather about celebrating Cebu's unique contributions to the country and exploring the concept of self-determination through a creative, symbolic project.

By embracing its rich past and leveraging its modern infrastructure, Cebu could become a successful and influential micronation on the global stage, albeit without formal recognition.

CHAPTER 2

THE VISION FOR A CEBUANO MICRONATION

Defining the Vision: A Cebuano Republic or Principality?

When creating a micronation, one of the first decisions to make is the form of government. For Cebu, two popular models could be a republic or a principality. Each of these models has its pros and cons:

Republic

A republic would be governed by elected officials, similar to the existing political structure of the Philippines, but with a focus on localized governance. In a republic, a president or prime minister would be chosen by the citizens, along with a parliament or legislative body. This system promotes democratic values and emphasizes citizen participation.

Principality

A principality is a micronation ruled by a monarch, such as a prince or princess, with the possibility of maintaining ceremonial power while the day-to-day governance is handled by appointed officials or ministers. This could be a symbolic nod to Cebu's precolonial history, where local chiefs, or "datus," governed. The title could be used to inspire a sense of continuity with the past.

The Purpose of a Cebuano Micronation

What should be the primary purpose of the Cebuano micronation? Defining its mission is key to shaping its identity. Several potential purposes could drive this endeavor:

Cultural Preservation

The micronation could focus on the preservation and promotion of Cebuano culture, language, and history. By establishing a symbolic state, it would celebrate the rich heritage of the region and ensure that future generations remain connected to their roots.

Local Autonomy

Another purpose could be to symbolically advocate for greater local autonomy within the Philippines. While actual secession is not possible, a micronation could serve as a political statement about the need for more regional control over economic and political affairs.

Creative and Artistic Expression

The micronation could be a space for creative exploration, where citizens participate in an artistic project that blends governance, culture, and identity into a unique expression of nationhood. This could draw international attention and attract visitors interested in the concept of micronations.

Identifying the Values and Goals: Independence, Autonomy, or Cultural Preservation?

The values and goals of the micronation should reflect the identity of Cebu and its people. Whether a micronation is driven by the desire for symbolic independence, cultural preservation, or a push for greater autonomy, these goals need to be clearly defined.

Independence

This would be purely symbolic, as Cebu cannot legally secede from the Philippines. However, a "declaration of independence" could be an important symbolic act, promoting a sense of local pride.

Autonomy

A more realistic goal might be advocating for further autonomy within the Philippines. This could include calls for greater control over local governance, tax policies, and public services.

Cultural Preservation

The micronation should prioritize the protection and promotion of Cebuano traditions, language, and history, thereby ensuring the celebration and maintenance of Cebu's unique identity.

National Motto, Symbols, and Philosophies

Every nation, even a micronation, needs symbols that encapsulate its identity and vision. These could include:

National Motto

The National Motto is a concise statement that embodies the values of the nation. For Cebu, something like "Kalig-on ug Kahayag (Strength and Light) could symbolize resilience and hope.

National Flag

A flag that incorporates Cebuano symbols, such as the Sinulog festival's cultural motifs, could be designed to represent the micronation. The colors blue (for the sea), gold (for prosperity), and green (for the land) might be symbolic choices.

Philosophies

The core philosophies of the micronation would shape its governance and culture. These could include concepts like sustainability, community engagement, and pride in Cebuano heritage.

Chapter 3

Legal Foundations and Challenges

Understanding International Law and Philippine Sovereignty

Micronations occupy a legal limbo. Despite many declaring independence, neither the international community nor the larger states within which they are located recognize them. This is the first legal challenge any micronation faces.

In the context of Cebu, Philippine sovereignty is constitutionally protected, and no region can declare itself independent without facing legal consequences. The 1987 Philippine Constitution guarantees the unity and territorial integrity of the country, meaning Cebu's creation as a legally recognized nation-state would be impossible without violating national law.

Internationally, established states or organizations like the United Nations rarely acknowledge micronations. While some micronations, such as Sealand or Liberland, have attracted media attention, their existence is more symbolic than that of actual sovereign nations.

The Legality of Micronations: Limitations and Risks

Because Cebu is part of a sovereign state, the creation of a "Republic of Cebu" would likely face legal challenges if it sought actual independence. Laws on sedition, rebellion, or treason could view any attempt at secession as a violation. Therefore, the micronation should be symbolic rather than an actual attempt to break away from the Philippines.

Keeping the project symbolic minimizes the risks of legal repercussions. A micronation that operates more as a cultural or creative project would not directly challenge Philippine law and would be more palatable to both the local and national governments.

Legal Precedents in Micronation Movements Worldwide

Many micronations around the world exist without legal recognition from their host countries. For example:

Sealand

Located on a World War II sea fort off the coast of England, Sealand declared independence in 1967. The British government and other nations still do not recognize Sealand, despite some international attention.

Liberland

Liberland is a libertarian micronation that was established in 2015 on disputed land between Serbia and Croatia. While it has issued passports and gained attention, it is not legally recognized.

These examples show that while micronations can declare sovereignty, they often operate outside the framework of international law, existing more as creative or ideological projects than legitimate states.

What Cebu's Constitution Would Like in a Micronation Context

A constitution would form the foundation of Cebu's micronation. This document could outline the principles of governance, the rights of citizens, and the structure of the government. A sample outline of the micronation's constitution might include:

Preamble

The preamble serves as a statement that reflects the micronation's values and mission, which include the preservation of Cebuano culture and the promotion of local governance.

Basic Principles

The basic principles include a symbolic declaration of sovereignty and a commitment to peaceful relations with the Philippines and other nations.

Government Structure

The document provides a comprehensive elucidation of the functioning of the government, encompassing the functions of leaders, legislative bodies, and the judiciary.

Citizen Rights and Duties

The section outlines the rights of citizens, which include freedom of speech, the right to vote, and the duty to preserve the nation's culture and environment.

Avoiding Legal Repercussions: Keeping It Symbolic

To avoid legal challenges, it is crucial that the Cebuano micronation remain a symbolic project. Its goals should focus on cultural preservation, local governance advocacy, and community building rather than outright secession. By framing the project as a celebration of Cebuano identity, the micronation can sidestep potential conflicts with the Philippine government while still achieving its objectives.

Chapter 4

Establishing Territory and Sovereignty

Defining Cebu's Territory: Urban Centers, Rural Areas, and the Islands

A crucial element in the creation of a micronation is the definition of its territory. Cebu's rich geography, consisting of its main island and surrounding smaller islands, offers various potential "territories" for the micronation. These could be divided into:

Urban Centers

Cities like Cebu City and Mandaue City could serve as symbolic capitals of the micronation. The urban landscape is crucial for demonstrating the region's modernity and economic strength.

Rural Areas

Cebu's rural regions could be designated as key territories for agriculture, cultural preservation, and sustainable development. These areas are crucial for preserving Cebu's unique cultural and natural heritage, and they could also function as centers for promoting traditional Cebuano farming, crafts, and customs.

The Islands

Cebu's smaller islands, including Mactan, Bantayan, and Camotes, could play significant roles in the micronation. Each island could represent a unique cultural or economic contribution to the micronation, including tourism, fishing, or marine conservation.

The micronation could symbolically assert its claim over the entire territory of the existing province of Cebu. However, for practical reasons, certain regions or even virtual spaces could be highlighted as core "sovereign" territory, especially if the project is positioned more as a cultural or artistic endeavor than a real political movement.

Negotiating Real and Symbolic Claims to Land

Micronations often face the challenge of asserting claims to actual land. Since the Philippines' national government maintains full control over its territory, any claim to land by a micronation would be symbolic rather than legally binding. To avoid legal conflicts, the micronation could focus on specific cultural or historical sites that are deeply connected to Cebu's heritage, such as Magellan's Cross, Fort San Pedro, or the Basilica del Santo Niño.

In some cases, private land could be designated as part of the micronation. For example, if private landowners in Cebu support the concept of the micronation, they could symbolically donate portions of their property to the project. These spaces could serve as headquarters or cultural hubs for the micronation.

Another option is to establish **virtual territories**. With the rise of digital platforms, a significant portion of the territory of the micronation could exist online. The virtual territory could include digital representations of landmarks in Cebu, online marketplaces, and spaces for citizens to gather, debate, and interact.

Creating Virtual Territories and Expanding Through Digital Platforms

Virtual micronations have become increasingly popular, with many existing primarily in the digital realm. For Cebu's micronation, creating a virtual territory could be a way to avoid the legal complexities of claiming real land while still maintaining a sense of community and sovereignty. Some ideas for virtual territory include:

A Virtual Capital City

Develop an online representation of Cebu City, complete with key landmarks, government buildings, and cultural institutions. Citizens could explore and interact with the virtual city, which would reinforce their sense of identity.

Online Citizenship Portals

Citizens could register online and access services such as voting, participating in discussions about governance, or contributing to cultural projects.

Digital Embassies

Establishing embassies on popular platforms like Discord, Reddit, or other forums would allow other micronations and supporters to engage diplomatically with Cebu.

By emphasizing digital infrastructure, the Cebuano micronation can engage with a broader audience, including the Cebuano diaspora, and expand its influence far beyond the physical borders of the island.

Managing Resources, Infrastructure, and the Environment in a Micronation

While a real-world micronation typically must manage physical resources, the Cebu micronation could focus on promoting sustainability, resource management, and ecological conservation as part of its mission. By promoting Cebu's natural beauty, the micronation can position itself as an advocate for environmental protection, similar to other micronations that emphasize green technology and ecological balance.

Resource management could focus on symbolic ownership of Cebu's natural resources, such as its forests, marine life, and beaches. Efforts to protect these resources could be a key part of the micronation's platform, encouraging environmental sustainability and ecotourism. The promotion of infrastructure projects within the symbolic micronation could focus on modern technology, such as renewable energy, waste management systems, and advanced public transport. These initiatives could highlight the forward-thinking nature of the micronation, with a focus on creating a sustainable future for all its citizens.

CHAPTER 5

GOVERNMENT STRUCTURE AND POLITICAL SYSTEMS

Choosing the Right Government for Cebu: Republic, Monarchy, or Federation?

The form of government for the Cebu micronation must reflect its values and mission. Different forms of governance come with different implications for leadership, citizen participation, and political structure.

Republic

In a republic, the government is headed by elected officials. Citizens would vote for their president or prime minister, and representatives would serve in a legislative body. This form of government would ensure citizen participation and a democratic decision-making process.

Monarchy

A monarchical system, with a prince or princess as the symbolic head of state, could reflect Cebu's precolonial roots. The monarch could have a mostly ceremonial role, similar to European constitutional monarchies, with elected officials managing the day-to-day affairs.

Federation

A federation would divide Cebu into regions or provinces, with each area having a certain degree of autonomy. This system would allow for local governance within different parts of the micronation, reflecting the diversity of Cebu's urban and rural areas.

Roles of Leadership: President, Monarch, or Council of Elders?

Regardless of the type of government, leadership roles must be defined clearly, ensuring that the structure of power within the micronation is balanced and representative of its citizens.

President

In a republic model, the president could serve as the head of state and government, elected by the citizens or representatives. The president would lead the executive branch and be responsible for overseeing day-to-day governance, international relations, and the implementation of laws passed by the legislative body.

Monarch

If the micronation adopts a monarchical system, the monarch (king, queen, prince, or princess) could serve as the symbolic head of state, representing the continuity of Cebuano traditions. While the monarch may not have political power, they could act as a figurehead, promoting Cebu's cultural identity and unity.

Council of Elders

A council of elders or a governing body composed of respected leaders could also lead the micronation. This system, inspired by indigenous governance structures, could involve elders or community leaders guiding the nation through consensus-based decision-making, reflecting Cebuano values of wisdom and collective governance.

How to Run a Micronation's Political System: Elections, Appointments, and Referendums

A functioning political system is necessary for any micronation to create a sense of legitimacy, even if it's symbolic. There are several mechanisms that could be employed to run the government in Cebu's micronation:

Elections

Citizens could elect representatives, ministers, or a president through free and fair elections. This could happen on an annual or biennial basis. To keep the micronation accessible and engaging, voting could be done through an online platform, allowing citizens from around the world to participate in the political process.

Appointments

Some leadership roles, such as those in the judiciary or advisory councils, could be appointed based on merit, experience, or contributions to the micronation. This system could ensure that key positions are held by individuals who are committed to the vision of the micronation.

Referendums

On major issues, referendums could be held to allow citizens to directly participate in decision-making. These could include decisions on constitutional amendments, laws, or symbolic declarations about Cebu's sovereignty.

The political system of the micronation should prioritize transparency, citizen engagement, and inclusivity, ensuring that all citizens feel they have a voice in how the nation is governed.

Cebuano Micronation Laws and Legal Frameworks

The legal framework of the micronation will be one of its most important documents. These laws would define the rights of citizens, the responsibilities of the government, and the general conduct of the nation's activities.

Though symbolic, the legal system could mirror real-world models while adapting them to the unique needs of the micronation. Some basic laws that could be included are:

Citizenship Laws

Rules governing who can become a citizen, including application procedures and responsibilities.

Rights of Citizens

A Bill of Rights or similar document that outlines the freedoms and protections guaranteed to citizens, such as freedom of speech, equality, and the right to cultural expression.

Governance Laws

Laws that define the responsibilities of the executive, legislative, and judicial branches, along with guidelines for elections, appointments, and the passage of new laws.

The legal framework could also include traditional Cebuano laws and customs, ensuring that the culture and history of the region are reflected in the micronation's governance.

Creating a Judiciary and Enforcement System for the Micronation

Even in a symbolic micronation, a judiciary is essential to maintain the rule of law. The judiciary could be composed of a small panel of judges or elders tasked with interpreting the micronation's constitution and resolving disputes among citizens.

The creation of law enforcement, while symbolic, could emphasize community policing and self-regulation. The micronation could encourage citizens to uphold its laws, resolving minor infractions through dialogue and mediation instead of punitive measures.

While the micronation might not need a full-fledged police force, the idea of symbolic law enforcement—such as "Cultural Guardians" tasked with protecting Cebu's heritage—could add a layer of fun and engagement for citizens.

Chapter 6

Citizenship and Civic Engagement

Defining Cebuano Citizenship: Who Qualifies, and How to Apply?

Citizenship in the micronation could be open to anyone who shares a love for Cebu, its culture, and its values.

The process for becoming a citizen should be simple and inclusive, allowing people from different backgrounds to join the micronation, whether they live in Cebu or are part of the Cebuano diaspora.

To apply for citizenship, prospective citizens could be asked to complete a short online form, pledging their support for the micronation's mission and values.

The micronation could also offer dual citizenship, allowing people to remain citizens of their home countries while symbolically supporting Cebu's micronation project.

Eligibility for citizenship could include:

Cebuanos by Birth

Anyone born in Cebu or with Cebuano heritage would automatically qualify for citizenship.

Cultural Citizens

People who have lived in Cebu or who have demonstrated a commitment to preserving Cebuano culture could also be eligible.

Honorary Citizens

Honorary citizenship could be awarded to individuals from outside Cebu who contribute to the micronation's mission, such as artists, scholars, or supporters of the project.

Creating Citizenship Documents (Passports, IDs, Birth Certificates)

One of the exciting aspects of a micronation is creating official documents for its citizens. Although other states would not recognize these documents, they could serve as powerful symbols of belonging and identity within the micronation.

Passports

The micronation could issue symbolic passports to its citizens. These could be designed with Cebuano motifs and issued to citizens upon application, serving as a tangible connection to the micronation.

ID Cards

Citizen ID cards could be used for symbolic purposes, such as voting in elections or accessing certain online platforms exclusive to citizens.

Birth Certificates

Symbolic birth certificates could be issued for new citizens, celebrating their entry into the micronation. This could be a particularly fun way to engage families or children in the project.

Rights and Duties of Citizens in the Micronation

Being a citizen of the Cebu micronation would come with both rights and responsibilities. These rights and duties could be enshrined in the micronation's constitution and could include:

Rights:

- Freedom of speech expression

- The right to participate the governance of the micronation

- The right to preserve promote Cebuano culture

- The right to protection and access to Cebu's natural heritage

Duties:

- Respecting the laws customs of the micronation

- Promoting Cebuano values, language, and traditions

- Contributing to themicronation's sustainability initiatives

- Supporting local international diplomatic efforts, if applicable

Engaging Citizens in Governance: Voting Systems Representation

Active citizen engagement is crucial for the success of the micronation. To encourage participation, the micronation could develop an online voting system where citizens can cast votes in national elections, referendums, or even symbolic international relations decisions.

Elections

Regular elections could be held for leadership positions, such as president, prime minister, or council members. Citizens could vote online to choose their representatives and hold them accountable.

Referendums

Citizens could participate in referendums to voice their opinions on major issues like constitutional amendments or symbolic declarations.

Additionally, representation within the government could be based on **regions** (urban vs. rural Cebu) or **sectors** (cultural, environmental, and economic sectors), ensuring that all parts of the micronation have a voice in governance.

Building a Civic Identity: Festivals, National Holidays, and Cultural Institutions

One of the most exciting aspects of building a micronation is creating a unique **civic identity** that resonates with citizens. Festivals, national holidays, and cultural institutions are vital to promoting that identity.

Festivals

The micronation could celebrate Cebu's existing festivals, like the Sinulog Festival, as national holidays. In addition, new symbolic festivals could be created, celebrating milestones in the micronation's development or key moments in Cebuano history.

National Holidays

Important dates in Cebuano history could be commemorated as national holidays in the micronation, with citizens participating in symbolic events and celebrations. These could include the founding of the micronation, the anniversary of Magellan's arrival, or days dedicated to important cultural figures.

Cultural Institutions

Creating museums, libraries, or archives, either physically or virtually, could help promote Cebuano heritage. These institutions could serve as cultural hubs, fostering creativity, knowledge, and education within the micronation.

CHAPTER 7

ECONOMY AND FINANCIAL SYSTEMS

Designing a Micronation Economy: Currency or Barter System?

A functional economy is an essential part of any micronation, even if symbolic. For Cebu's micronation, several models could be explored:

Currency

The micronation could create its own symbolic currency, used for exchanges within the community or at official events. The currency could reflect Cebuano culture and history, with designs showcasing important local symbols, historical figures, or landmarks.

Barter System

Alternatively, the micronation could embrace a barter system, where citizens exchange goods and services rather than relying on currency. This system would emphasize sustainability and community cooperation, aligning with Cebu's focus on preserving its environment and culture.

Creating Currency: Design, Value, and Use

Cebu's unique culture and history, while also serving a practical purpose within the micronation. The currency could be used in symbolic transactions, events, or internal trade systems, providing citizens with a tangible connection to the micronation's economy. Here are some steps to consider when creating the currency:

Design

The currency could feature iconic Cebuano symbols, such as the Magellan's Cross, Lapu-Lapu, or the Basilica del Santo Niño. The use of vibrant colors and traditional Cebuano patterns would make the currency both a work of art and a functional tool. Denominations could range from smaller units for everyday symbolic use (such as 1, 5, or 10 Cebuano pesos) to higher denominations for ceremonial purposes.

Value

While the currency would not be officially tied to the global economy, it could be given a symbolic value, perhaps tied to virtual or community-based transactions within the micronation. The currency could be used to "purchase" cultural items, participate in events, or support internal projects. The value of the currency could also be tied to specific aspects of Cebuano culture, such as earning it through contributing to local traditions or cultural preservation.

Use

The currency could be used in both physical and digital form. In physical form, it could be printed or minted and distributed to citizens for ceremonial use. In digital form, it could be used on an online platform for purchasing symbolic items, voting in elections, or contributing to national causes.

This integration of physical and digital currency would help engage a broader audience, including those living outside Cebu.

How to Sustain an Economy: Trade, Tourism, and Exports

Even in a symbolic micronation, an economic foundation is necessary to support cultural and civic projects. While traditional economic systems such as trade, tourism, and exports are more applicable to recognized nations, they could still be adapted to a micronation context for Cebu:

Trade

The micronation could engage in symbolic trade with other micronations or local businesses, exchanging culturally significant items such as handcrafted goods, local produce, or even symbolic tokens of Cebuano heritage. This trade could highlight Cebu's rich tradition of craftsmanship and agriculture while fostering relationships with similar projects worldwide.

Tourism

Cebu is already a popular tourist destination, known for its beautiful beaches, historical sites, and vibrant festivals. The micronation could create symbolic "tourist packages" or events that draw visitors into its cultural and symbolic narrative.

Annual Programs

Events like Micronation Days or Cultural Exchange Programs could be held annually, inviting tourists to experience Cebu's micronation through guided tours, educational seminars, or artistic exhibitions. Symbolic passports or stamps could be offered to tourists as a memorable part of their experience.

Exports

Cebu's rich tradition of exporting goods, such as furniture, handicrafts, and agricultural products, could be celebrated within the micronation by creating partnerships with local artisans and businesses.

The micronation could promote local craftsmanship by showcasing and "exporting" symbolic items like stamps, coins, and souvenirs. These could be sold both physically and online, allowing the micronation to generate revenue for cultural and civic projects.

Building Institutions: National Banks, Taxes, and Revenue Generation

Though primarily symbolic, the creation of financial institutions within the micronation would add to its legitimacy and operational efficiency.

National Bank

A symbolic National Bank of Cebu could be established to manage the micronation's currency, fund national projects, and regulate symbolic transactions. This bank could also serve as a cultural institution, promoting Cebuano traditions of craftsmanship and trade. It could also offer loans or grants to citizens to support community projects, art, or entrepreneurial endeavors.

Taxes

Citizens of the micronation could pay symbolic taxes to support national projects, such as the preservation of cultural sites or the organization of events. These taxes would not be monetary in the traditional sense but could be paid in terms of time, skills, or symbolic contributions, such as participating in cultural festivals, volunteering for civic duties, or contributing to environmental projects.

Revenue Generation

In addition to symbolic taxes and trade, the micronation could generate revenue through merchandise sales, events, or online platforms. The sale of national symbols, such as flags, coins, or art, could help fund cultural initiatives, while entry fees to certain events could also provide a source of income. Additionally, partnerships with local businesses and tourism agencies could help sustain the micronation's projects.

Exploring Economies: Cryptocurrency and E-Government

With the rise of cryptocurrency and e-governance, the Cebu micronation could explore innovative economic models that go beyond traditional frameworks. By integrating blockchain technology and creating its own cryptocurrency, the micronation could engage with a global audience interested in new financial systems.

Cryptocurrency

A Cebuano cryptocurrency, called something like "CebuCoin, could be created and used for virtual transactions within the micronation's online platforms. This cryptocurrency could be used for purchasing digital goods, donating to cultural projects, or investing in community-driven initiatives. Additionally, the use of blockchain technology would allow for transparent and secure transactions, promoting trust and engagement among citizens and participants.

E-Government

The micronation could also establish a digital government platform where citizens can vote in elections, participate in national discussions, or submit proposals for new projects. This platform could include digital IDs, online voting, and virtual forums for citizen participation. E-governance would make the micronation accessible to people around the world, including members of the Cebuano diaspora, allowing them to participate in national affairs no matter their location.

CHAPTER 8

DIPLOMATIC RELATIONS AND FOREIGN POLICY

Diplomatic Relations with the Philippines and Other Nations

While the Cebu micronation would be a symbolic project, maintaining positive relationships with the Philippine government and other nations would be crucial to its success. The micronation would not seek independence but rather a cultural creative space that promotes Cebuano heritage and identity.

Diplomacy with the Philippines

It would be important to maintain a cooperative and respectful relationship with the Philippine government. The micronation could emphasize its symbolic nature, ensuring that it does not challenge the Philippines' sovereignty or legal framework. By positioning itself as a cultural project, the micronation could even work with local and national governments to promote tourism, cultural preservation, and regional pride.

Relations with Other Micronations

The Cebu micronation could establish symbolic diplomatic relations with other micronations around the world. Many micronations, such as Sealand or Liberland, have formed symbolic alliances, treaties, or cooperative projects with one another. By participating in the micronation community, Cebu could share its culture, learn from other projects, and gain international recognition within this unique sphere.

Engaging with the International Micronation Community

There is an entire community of micronations around the world, each with its own vision, governance system, and cultural identity. By engaging with this community, Cebu's micronation could gain valuable insights, partnerships, and symbolic recognition. Some ways to engage include:

Attending Micronation Conferences

Occasionally, micronations organize conferences or summits where leaders and citizens gather to discuss topics of shared interest. The Cebu micronation could send representatives to these events, building relationships with other projects and exchanging ideas.

Forming Alliances

Alliances could be formed with other micronations that share similar values or goals. For example, an alliance focused on cultural preservation, environmental protection, or local autonomy could unite Cebu with other like-minded projects.

Micronation Diplomacy

Symbolic treaties or agreements could be signed with other micronations, focusing on shared goals like tourism promotion, cultural exchanges, or environmental protection. These diplomatic gestures would further solidify Cebu's place in the global micronation community.

The Role of Treaties and Alliances in Micronation Diplomacy

While legally binding treaties are not possible for micronations, symbolic treaties and alliances can serve to reinforce the legitimacy of the project. These agreements could be focused on cultural, environmental, or social goals, promoting collaboration between like-minded projects.

Cultural Treaties

Agreements with other micronations focused on cultural exchange could help spread Cebu's rich traditions across the world. These treaties could involve cultural ambassadors, art exchanges, or joint festivals that celebrate the diversity of micronations.

Environmental Alliances

Cebu's commitment to environmental sustainability could be shared with other micronations through treaties focused on green technology, marine conservation, or sustainable development. These alliances would emphasize the micronation's role as a responsible global actor, even within a symbolic framework.

Establishing Embassies Consulates (Symbolically Digitally)

A micronation can further establish its presence on the global stage by setting up symbolic embassies or consulates in friendly countries or other micronations. These could take the form of physical spaces, such as dedicated rooms or sections of buildings, or digital embassies, located on websites or social media platforms.

Physical Embassies

While unlikely in reality, symbolic embassies could be created in friendly micronations that support the project. These embassies could serve as cultural hubs where visitors can learn more about Cebu's heritage, participate in events, or receive symbolic "consular" services.

Digital Embassies

The easier and more accessible option is creating digital embassies. These could be dedicated websites or social media accounts that represent the Cebu micronation to the outside world. These platforms could host diplomatic announcements, cultural exchanges, or even virtual visa applications for those who want to symbolically visit or engage with the micronation. Digital embassies could also provide a space for international dialogue, where other micronations, supporters, and citizens of the world can interact with Cebu's leaders and citizens.

Promoting Cebu as a Peaceful, Independent Entity

One of the micronation's key messages would be its promotion as a peaceful entity focused on cultural preservation, education, and sustainability. By emphasizing its non-confrontational and cooperative nature, Cebu's micronation could garner positive attention and avoid conflicts with both local and national governments. Here are some ways to promote Cebu's peaceful independence:

Cultural Diplomacy

Cebu's rich history and vibrant culture could serve as the primary focus of its diplomacy. Cultural exchanges, events, and partnerships with other nations, organizations, and institutions could reinforce the micronation's mission as a hub of Cebuano heritage.

Environmental Leadership

By positioning itself as a leader in environmental protection and sustainability, Cebu could gain international attention. Efforts to preserve marine life, promote ecotourism, and implement green technology could be highlighted in its diplomatic efforts, making the micronation a model for responsible global citizenship.

Peaceful Coexistence

Public statements and treaties could reaffirm the micronation's commitment to peaceful coexistence with the Philippines and other nations. By focusing on cultural rather than political autonomy, Cebu could ensure that its project remains symbolic and non-disruptive, fostering positive relationships with surrounding regions.

Chapter 9

Cultural Preservation and National Identity

Celebrating Cebu's Rich History: Precolonial Times to Present Day

One of the primary missions of the Cebu micronation would be the preservation and celebration of its rich history. This history spans from precolonial times, when Cebu was a major trading hub in Southeast Asia, through the Spanish colonial period, and into the modern era of Cebu's development as a key economic and cultural center of the Philippines.

The micronation could establish historical programs and cultural education initiatives to ensure that both citizens and visitors understand the significance of Cebu's past. Some initiatives could include:

National History Day

An annual event celebrating key moments in Cebu's history, such as Lapu-Lapu's resistance to Magellan's forces and Cebu's role in the establishment of Catholicism in the Philippines.

Museums and Archives

The micronation could fund symbolic museums or online archives that preserve and display historical documents, artifacts, and stories from Cebu's past. These institutions would serve as a resource for historians, students, and citizens interested in the region's history.

Historical Tours and Events

Organizing guided tours of Cebu's historical sites, such as Fort San Pedro, Magellan's Cross, and Basilica del Santo Niño, would help keep the micronation's history alive. These tours could be led by cultural ambassadors or local historians, offering both citizens and tourists a deeper understanding of Cebu's heritage.

Language, Arts, and Traditions: How to Promote Cebuano Culture

A key aspect of the Cebu micronation's identity would be its promotion of Cebuano language, arts, and traditions. By fostering a deep connection to the island's unique culture, the micronation could strengthen the sense of national identity among its citizens.

Language Preservation

Cebuano, one of the major languages of the Philippines, could be promoted as the official language of the micronation. This would involve encouraging citizens to speak Cebuano in official events and daily life, as well as establishing language education programs for those who are not fluent. The micronation could also fund language preservation initiatives, such as creating digital archives of Cebuano literature, poetry, and folklore.

Artistic Expression

Cebu's thriving art scene could be supported through national programs that fund artists, musicians, and performers who celebrate Cebuano identity. The micronation could host art exhibitions, music festivals, and theater productions, with an emphasis on traditional forms of Cebuano art alongside modern interpretations.

Cultural Traditions

Festivals, dances, and religious celebrations such as Sinulog could be central to the micronation's calendar. These events would not only serve as a way to bring citizens together but also as an opportunity to showcase Cebu's rich traditions to the world. We could encourage citizens to participate in these events by wearing traditional clothing, preparing Cebuano dishes, and learning Cebuano dances.

Creating National Symbols: Flags, Emblems, and Anthems

Every micronation needs symbols that represent its identity. These symbols would serve as a point of pride for citizens and a way to communicate the values and heritage of the micronation to the world.

Flag

The flag of the Cebu micronation could be designed with Cebuano symbols and colors. A proposed design might include blue to represent the surrounding seas, green for the island's lush nature, and gold to symbolize prosperity. A central icon, such as Magellan's Cross or an image of Lapu-Lapu, could represent Cebu's resilience and history.

Emblem

An official emblem or coat of arms could be created to represent the micronation in official documents and events. This emblem could combine elements of Cebu's rich history, such as references to its indigenous roots, Spanish influence, and modern-day development.

Anthem

A national anthem could be composed in Cebuano, with lyrics that reflect the values of the micronation—pride in heritage, unity among citizens, and a commitment to cultural preservation. This anthem could be performed at national events, festivals, and official ceremonies, becoming a symbol of collective identity for the citizens.

Institutionalizing Cultural Practices: Schools, Museums, and Festivals

To ensure the survival and flourishing of Cebuano culture, the micronation could create institutions that actively promote and support cultural practices:

Schools and Educational Programs

A network of schools or educational programs could be established to teach the next generation about Cebu's history, language, and cultural traditions. These schools could focus on both academic education and cultural immersion, ensuring that students have a strong connection to their Cebuano identity. Online educational platforms could extend these programs to the broader Cebuano diaspora.

Museums and Cultural Centers

Physical or digital museums could serve as the custodians of Cebuano heritage. These museums would house historical artifacts, artworks, and interactive exhibits that tell the story of Cebu's past. Cultural centers could also be created to host workshops, performances, and festivals, serving as a community hub for citizens.

Festivals and Celebrations

National festivals would be central to the life of the micronation, with events such as Sinulog taking on an official status. These festivals could serve as a way for citizens to come together and celebrate their shared identity, with parades, music, dance, and traditional food playing key roles.

Ensuring Cultural Continuity: Supporting Cebuano Literature, Music, and Dance

Cultural continuity is vital to the success of any nation, and Cebu's micronation would need to actively support its artistic traditions to ensure that they remain vibrant for future generations.

Literature

The micronation could sponsor writing competitions, literary festivals, and publications that promote Cebuano literature. It could also fund translations of Cebuano works into other languages, ensuring that the nation's stories and voices reach a global audience.

Music

National programs that support musicians and songwriters could celebrate Cebuano music, both traditional and modern. The creation of a national orchestra or choir could provide a platform for showcasing Cebuano music at events and festivals.

Dance

Schools could teach traditional dances like those performed during Sinulog and showcase them at national events. The micronation could also fund dance troupes that travel internationally to share Cebu's cultural heritage with the world.

By actively investing in these cultural initiatives, the micronation would ensure that Cebuano traditions are passed down through generations, creating a sense of continuity and shared identity.

CHAPTER 10

DEFENSE AND SECURITY IN A MICRONATION

Establishing a Micronation Defense Policy: Military or Peaceful Coexistence?

While a traditional military would not be necessary for a symbolic micronation, a clear defense policy could still be established to promote peace and security within the community. The focus of Cebu's micronation could be on peaceful coexistence, prioritizing diplomacy, cultural engagement, and conflict resolution over militarization.

Peaceful Coexistence

The micronation could issue a formal declaration that it seeks to exist peacefully alongside the Philippines and other nations. This declaration could emphasize Cebu's role as a cultural project rather than a political entity seeking sovereignty. By adopting a non-aggressive stance, the micronation could foster positive relationships both locally and internationally.

National Defense Policy

Symbolically, the micronation could create a defense policy that focuses on cultural defense—the protection and promotion of Cebuano identity, traditions, and language. Instead of military force, the micronation would "defend" itself through cultural diplomacy, educational initiatives, and environmental conservation.

Creating a Symbolic Army or Militia

While a military force would not be necessary, some micronations create symbolic armies or militias as a form of national pride and community engagement. For Cebu's micronation, a symbolic Cultural Guard or Green Militia could be created with a focus on cultural preservation and environmental protection.

Cultural Guard

This could be a symbolic body of citizens who pledge to protect Cebu's cultural heritage, acting as ambassadors of the nation's traditions and values. Members of the Cultural Guard could participate in national festivals, represent the micronation at international cultural events, and lead initiatives to preserve historical landmarks, language, and customs. Their "duties" would be primarily ceremonial, with the focus on raising awareness about Cebu's heritage and strengthening national pride.

Green Militia

Another option could be the creation of a symbolic Green Militia, dedicated to environmental protection and sustainability. This group could consist of volunteers who work on projects such as tree planting, marine conservation, and cleanup drives around Cebu's natural attractions. The Green Militia would serve as a reminder of the micronation's commitment to protecting its environment, positioning itself as a leader in environmental sustainability.

Cybersecurity Digital Sovereignty

In an increasingly digital world, protecting a micronation's online presence is essential. As much of Cebu's micronation could exist in virtual spaces, such as websites and social media platforms, a clear cybersecurity policy would be necessary to safeguard its digital assets and citizens' personal information.

Digital Sovereignty

The micronation could establish policies to ensure its websites, platforms, and digital infrastructure are secure from hacking, misinformation, or sabotage. This could involve partnering with cybersecurity experts or establishing a small team of digital guardians who monitor and protect the micronation's online presence.

Secure Communication

For government operations and citizen engagement, the micronation could implement encrypted communications for online voting, e-governance, and sensitive diplomatic exchanges. This would foster trust among citizens and create a sense of privacy and security within the micronation.

Managing Security: Crime Prevention, Law Enforcement, and Justice

Though crime would not be a significant concern in a symbolic micronation, establishing a justice system and mechanisms for managing internal conflicts would still be beneficial. These systems would help maintain order, promote fairness, and ensure that all citizens are treated equally under the micronation's laws.

Law Enforcement

While a full-scale police force is unnecessary, a symbolic body, such as the Cebuano Guardians of Peace, could be established to maintain order and uphold the micronation's values. Their role could be primarily focused on educating citizens about the micronation's laws and mediating disputes between citizens in a peaceful and constructive manner.

Justice System

A simple judicial system could be established to resolve conflicts and enforce the micronation's laws. A council of elders or appointed judges could serve as the arbiters of justice, ensuring that decisions are fair and rooted in Cebuano traditions. Citizens who break symbolic laws could face consequences such as community service or temporary restrictions from certain privileges, such as voting in national elections.

Protecting the Micronation from External and Internal Threats

While the micronation's existence would likely face little resistance, a proactive approach to protecting its sovereignty (symbolic or otherwise) would enhance its legitimacy and sustainability.

External Threats

Since the micronation would operate symbolically, the primary threats would come from external entities trying to undermine its mission or credibility. These could include cyberattacks, misinformation campaigns, or attempts to delegitimize its cultural mission. To combat these threats, the micronation could rely on public diplomacy, transparency, and cybersecurity measures to defend itself.

Internal Conflicts

Managing internal conflicts, such as disagreements between citizens or between government officials, would require the establishment of effective conflict resolution mechanisms. The micronation could use mediation and dialogue to resolve disputes, with an emphasis on maintaining community harmony and cooperation. A citizens' tribunal or ombudsman could serve as a neutral body to investigate and resolve internal conflicts.

Chapter 11

Tourism and International Recognition

Using Tourism as a Tool for Micronation Visibility and Income

Tourism is already a major industry in Cebu, and leveraging this for the micronation could help promote its cultural and symbolic initiatives. The micronation could establish a tourism board to oversee the development of tourism-related projects and activities, bringing in visitors who are curious about its unique status and its cultural offerings.

Micronation Tours

The micronation could offer tours of symbolic landmarks, such as historical sites, museums, or national parks, giving visitors an in-depth look at Cebu's heritage and the micronation's vision. These tours could include storytelling sessions, performances of traditional music and dance, and culinary experiences featuring Cebuano dishes.

Tourist Passports and Visas

As a fun and symbolic way to engage visitors, the micronation could issue tourist passports or visas that allow people to "enter" the micronation. These documents could be stamped when visitors attend cultural events or visit important landmarks, making for a unique souvenir and further immersing tourists in the micronation experience.

Cultural and Environmental Tours

The micronation could also focus on ecotourism and cultural heritage tourism, offering guided tours to Cebu's beaches, mountains, and islands, as well as workshops on traditional crafts, cuisine, or language. These initiatives would align with the micronation's goals of promoting sustainability and cultural preservation while also providing a source of income.

Creating National Landmarks, Monuments, and Museums

Establishing national landmarks and monuments would give the micronation's citizens and visitors a tangible connection to its history and values. These could be physical or symbolic sites that represent important moments in Cebu's history or embody the micronation's principles of cultural pride and autonomy.

National Monuments

Monuments could be built to commemorate key historical figures, such as Lapu-Lapu, or important events in Cebu's history, such as the Battle of Mactan or the introduction of Catholicism. These monuments would serve as focal points for national celebrations and cultural events.

National Museums

National museums could be established to house important artifacts, documents, and artworks related to Cebu's history, culture, and the micronation's development. These museums could offer interactive exhibits, guided tours, and educational programs to help visitors and citizens alike understand the depth of Cebuano heritage.

Natural Landmarks

Cebu's natural beauty could also be recognized through the creation of national parks or heritage sites, protecting key areas such as coral reefs, beaches, and forests. These landmarks could be part of the micronation's tourism strategy, promoting ecotourism and sustainable development.

Promoting Cebu's Micronation Status to Attract Visitors

By leveraging its unique micronation status, Cebu could attract tourists not only from the Philippines but also from around the world. Promoting the micronation's cultural initiatives, festivals, and natural beauty would help position it as a top destination for those seeking a meaningful travel experience.

Marketing Campaigns

A marketing campaign could be launched to promote the micronation's identity, focusing on its cultural richness, historical significance, and natural wonders. Social media, websites, and travel blogs could be used to spread the word, drawing visitors interested in both the uniqueness of a micronation and the beauty of Cebu.

Partnerships with Travel Agencies

The micronation could partner with local and international travel agencies to offer specialized tours and packages that include visits to the micronation's landmarks, festivals, and events. By creating a comprehensive experience, visitors would feel they are truly part of the micronation's cultural and symbolic journey.

Hosting International Events, Summits, or Competitions

To further promote Cebu's micronation and engage with the global community, the micronation could host international events that draw attention to its cultural, environmental, or diplomatic initiatives.

Cultural Festivals

The micronation could invite performers, artists, and cultural ambassadors from other micronations and countries to participate in annual cultural festivals. These events could showcase Cebuano traditions while providing a platform for global cultural exchange.

Environmental Summits

Given Cebu's emphasis on sustainability, the micronation could host environmental summits focused on marine conservation, sustainable tourism, and climate change. These summits could attract environmental leaders, researchers, and policymakers from around the world, elevating Cebu's status as a global leader in sustainability.

Micronation Competitions

Symbolic competitions, such as the Micronation Games, could be organized where citizens of various micronations compete in friendly athletic or cultural contests. These events could build camaraderie between micronations while providing an engaging and entertaining way to celebrate cultural identity.

How to Gain Recognition (Symbolic) from Other Micronations and Global Movements

Although it is unlikely for a micronation to receive official recognition from other countries or international bodies, Cebu's project could still pursue symbolic recognition from other micronations and global movements that advocate for autonomy, cultural preservation, or sustainability.

Micronation Alliances

By building diplomatic relationships with other micronations, Cebu could become part of a larger micronation alliance, which could help raise its profile and increase its legitimacy within the global micronation community.

Recognition from Cultural Organizations

Cebu's micronation could also seek recognition from cultural and environmental organizations that align with its goals. Partnerships with UNESCO, international heritage groups, or ecotourism organizations could provide further legitimacy and support for the micronation's mission.

Participation in Global Movements

The micronation could participate in global movements focused on sustainability, cultural preservation, and regional autonomy. By aligning itself with these causes, Cebu's micronation could gain visibility and support from both citizens and organizations around the world.

Chapter 12

Education, Science, & Technology in a Micronation

Establishing a National Education System: Promoting Heritage and Knowledge

One of the core responsibilities of Cebu's micronation would be the establishment of an educational system that not only promotes general knowledge but also emphasizes the importance of Cebuano culture, language, and history. The micronation's national education system could focus on several key areas:

Cultural Education

Classes and workshops on Cebuano history, traditional crafts, language, and folklore could be integrated into all levels of education. These programs would ensure that younger generations grow up with a deep understanding of their cultural identity and heritage.

Language Programs

The Cebuano language could be made a core subject in all schools, with initiatives to promote fluency among citizens. Language programs could also include classes for nonnative speakers or visitors who wish to learn Cebuano.

STEM Education

In addition to cultural education, the micronation could emphasize the importance of science, technology, engineering, and mathematics (STEM) education. This would help the micronation remain innovative and forward-thinking, equipping students with the skills they need for the future.

Environmental Studies

Given the micronation's commitment to sustainability, schools could integrate environmental science and conservation into the curriculum. Students could learn about the importance of protecting Cebu's natural resources and ecosystems and engage in hands-on environmental projects such as tree planting or marine conservation.

Supporting Higher Education and Research

Beyond primary and secondary education, the micronation could also establish or partner with universities and research institutions to promote advanced learning and research in areas that are central to Cebu's identity and sustainability efforts.

Cebuano Heritage Studies

Higher education programs could focus on research in Cebuano history, archaeology, anthropology, and cultural studies. Scholars could explore Cebu's rich past and contribute to a greater understanding of its role in regional and global history.

Environmental Research

The micronation could fund research projects focused on marine biology, **renewable energy**, and **climate change**. By investing in environmental research, the micronation could position itself as a leader in sustainable development and environmental conservation in Southeast Asia.

Technology and Innovation Hubs

The creation of **technology hubs** or **innovation centers** could encourage citizens and students to develop new technologies that benefit the micronation. These hubs could focus on renewable energy, sustainable agriculture, and digital infrastructure.

Integrating Technology: E-Government and Digital Infrastructure

Technology could play a central role in how the micronation operates and engages with its citizens. As a symbolic micronation with potentially many citizens living outside Cebu, a robust e-government system would be essential.

E-Government

Citizens could engage with the micronation's government entirely online, using digital platforms for voting, submitting policy proposals, and accessing public services. This would create a seamless way for citizens to participate in governance, regardless of their physical location.

Smart Cities

The micronation could integrate smart city technology into its urban areas, promoting energy-efficient buildings, public transportation powered by renewable energy, and digital infrastructure for real-time monitoring of resources like water and electricity.

Broadband and Connectivity

Ensuring that citizens have access to high-speed internet and other communication technologies would be essential for promoting economic growth, education, and civic engagement. Expanding broadband access to rural areas would help bridge the digital divide and ensure that all citizens can participate in the digital economy.

National Initiatives for Science, Technology, and Innovation

To position itself as a forward-thinking entity, the micronation could launch national initiatives that encourage innovation in science and technology. These initiatives could be supported through government funding, public-private partnerships, or international collaborations.

Innovation Grants

The micronation could establish a program to offer grants to individuals, startups, and research institutions working on innovative projects in fields like renewable energy, sustainable agriculture, or marine conservation. These grants could help drive innovation and position Cebu as a leader in eco-friendly technology.

Tech Festivals and Hackathons

Hosting tech festivals or hackathons could engage both citizens and international innovators in solving real-world challenges facing the micronation. These events could focus on developing apps, products, or policies that support the micronation's goals of sustainability, cultural preservation, and digital governance.

Partnerships with Global Tech Leaders

The micronation could seek partnerships with international tech companies and research organizations to bring cutting-edge technology to Cebu. These collaborations could involve joint research projects, training programs for students, and the establishment of local tech hubs.

Developing an Education for Citizenship: Teaching Patriotism Responsibility

One of the most important aspects of the micronation's education system would be citizenship education. This would involve teaching students about their rights and responsibilities as citizens of the micronation and instilling a sense of pride and dedication to Cebu's culture and future.

Civic Education

Students could learn about the micronation's constitution, laws, and governance system. Lessons on civic responsibility, voting, and active participation in the community could help build a strong sense of citizenship.

Patriotism

Schools could promote national pride by teaching students about Cebu's rich history and the micronation's values. Celebrating national holidays, such as Independence Day or Cultural Preservation Day, could help promote solidarity among citizens.

Community Service

Part of citizenship education could include community service projects, where students engage in local environmental cleanups, cultural festivals, or social initiatives. These projects would help instill a sense of responsibility for both the micronation and the broader community.

Chapter 13

Environmental Sustainability & Resource Management

Protecting Cebu's Natural Beauty: Islands, Forests, and Marine Ecosystems

As a micronation rooted in sustainability, protecting Cebu's natural environment would be one of its top priorities. This could involve initiatives aimed at conserving Cebu's islands, forests, marine ecosystems, and other natural resources.

Marine Conservation

Cebu is home to some of the most beautiful coral reefs and marine biodiversity in the world. The micronation could establish marine protected areas around its islands, working to restore coral reefs, protect endangered species, and promote responsible tourism.

Programs could include partnerships with international marine conservation organizations as well as local research institutions.

Forest Conservation

Efforts to preserve Cebu's remaining forests could include reforestation projects, promoting sustainable forestry practices, and protecting wildlife habitats. Citizens could participate in tree-planting drives, while educational programs teach the importance of forest ecosystems to Cebu's environmental health.

Sustainable Tourism

The micronation could promote ecotourism as a way to support local economies while minimizing the environmental impact of tourism. Visitors could be encouraged to visit eco-friendly resorts, participate in environmental tours, and support sustainable businesses.

Creating Environmental Laws for Sustainable Development

The micronation's legal framework would include environmental laws that prioritize sustainability and resource conservation. These laws would ensure that the development of urban areas, agriculture, and industry in the micronation respects the natural environment.

Environmental Impact Assessments (EIA)

Any new development in the micronation could be required to undergo an EIA to evaluate its potential impact on the environment. Projects that fail to meet the micronation's strict environmental standards could be revised or rejected, ensuring that all development aligns with the goal of sustainability.

Green Building Codes

The micronation could adopt green building codes that require new construction to meet energy efficiency standards, use sustainable materials, and incorporate renewable energy sources like solar or wind power. These codes would help reduce the micronation's carbon footprint and promote eco-friendly urban development.

Sustainable Agriculture Laws

To promote food security while protecting the environment, the micronation could encourage organic farming and sustainable agricultural practices. Laws could limit the use of harmful pesticides and encourage the use of composting, crop rotation, and other environmentally friendly farming techniques.

Encouraging Technology and Renewable Energy in the Micronation

The micronation could position itself as a leader in green technology and renewable energy, focusing on reducing its carbon footprint and promoting innovation in sustainability.

Solar and Wind Power

The micronation could invest in solar panels, wind turbines, and other renewable energy sources to power its cities and rural areas. Citizens could be encouraged to install solar panels on their homes, and public buildings could be retrofitted with energy-efficient technologies.

Electric Public Transport

To reduce the micronation's reliance on fossil fuels, an electric public transportation system could be developed, including buses, trams, or bike-sharing programs. This system would be accessible to all citizens and promote eco-friendly commuting.

Green Technology Incubators

The micronation could establish green technology incubators to support startups and innovators working on sustainable products and solutions. These incubators could offer grants, mentorship, and access to state-of-the-art facilities to help entrepreneurs develop new technologies in renewable energy, water conservation, and waste management.

Building a Self-Sufficient Agricultural Sector

Food security would be a key concern for the micronation, and building a self-sufficient agricultural sector would help ensure that citizens have access to fresh, healthy, and locally sourced food.

Urban Farming

The micronation could promote urban farming initiatives, encouraging citizens to grow their own fruits, vegetables, and herbs in community gardens or on rooftops. These initiatives would not only provide fresh food but also create green spaces in urban areas.

Organic Farming

The micronation could support organic farming practices, helping farmers transition away from harmful chemicals and adopt sustainable methods that protect the soil and water supply. This could include the use of **composting**, crop rotation, and permaculture techniques, which would ensure that agriculture in the micronation remains sustainable and environmentally friendly. Organic farming initiatives could also promote food exports to other regions, boosting the micronation's economy while aligning with its environmental goals.

Hydroponics and Aquaponics

To maximize food production in limited space, the micronation could explore hydroponic and aquaponic farming systems. These methods use less water than traditional farming and could be set up in urban areas, helping to grow crops like leafy greens, herbs, and vegetables all year round.

Waste Management Conservation in the Micronation

Effective waste management and conservation would be critical to maintaining the micronation's commitment to sustainability. The government could establish a zero-waste policy that prioritizes recycling, composting, and responsible waste disposal.

Recycling Programs

The micronation could implement comprehensive recycling programs, encouraging citizens to separate their waste into recyclable and non-recyclable categories. Public bins for paper, plastic, glass, and metal could be set up throughout cities, and a central recycling facility could be established to process materials efficiently.

Composting Initiatives

Citizens and businesses could be encouraged to compost organic waste such as food scraps and plant material. The compost produced could be used in community gardens and farms, reducing the need for chemical fertilizers and creating a closed-loop system for organic waste.

Water Conservation

Given the importance of water as a vital resource, the micronation could focus on water conservation efforts, such as the installation of rainwater harvesting systems in homes and businesses. Citizens could also be educated on water-saving practices, such as reducing household water use, repairing leaks, and using greywater for irrigation.

Sustainable Packaging

The micronation could adopt regulations that require businesses to use biodegradable or recyclable packaging for products sold within the country. This would help reduce plastic waste and promote the use of eco-friendly materials.

CHAPTER 14

MICRONATION CHALLENGES AND HOW TO OVERCOME THEM

Legal and Diplomatic Obstacles: Managing Relations with the Philippine Government

One of the major challenges the micronation would face is navigating its legal and diplomatic relationship with the Philippine government. While the micronation would operate symbolically, it is important to ensure that its existence does not violate national laws or lead to conflicts with the authorities.

Clarifying the Micronation's Intent

To avoid legal complications, the leaders of the Cebu micronation could issue a public statement clarifying that the micronation is a cultural project rather than a political secessionist movement. Emphasizing its focus on heritage preservation and symbolic governance would help build positive relationships with both local and national governments.

Cooperation with Local Authorities

Building relationships with local officials in Cebu would be crucial for the micronation's success. The micronation could collaborate with local governments on shared goals, such as promoting tourism, preserving cultural sites, and supporting sustainability efforts. By demonstrating that it is a partner in these efforts, the micronation could ensure that it operates without opposition from authorities.

International Diplomacy

The micronation could also pursue symbolic international diplomacy with other micronations and organizations. While legal recognition is unlikely, symbolic alliances, treaties, and partnerships with other micronations could help the project gain legitimacy within the global micronation community.

Ensuring Community Engagement and Avoiding Citizen Apathy

Maintaining a strong sense of community and ensuring that citizens remain engaged with the micronation's activities is another potential challenge. To avoid apathy, the micronation would need to create meaningful opportunities for citizens to participate in national life.

Encouraging Active Participation

The micronation could hold regular town hall meetings, citizen forums, and online discussions where citizens can share their ideas and concerns. Engaging citizens in decision-making and governance would help foster a sense of ownership and pride in the micronation.

Organizing National Events

Cultural festivals, environmental cleanup days, and educational workshops could be held throughout the year to keep citizens engaged. By providing a variety of events that appeal to different interests, the micronation would ensure that citizens feel a strong connection to the community.

Rewarding Civic Participation

To further incentivize participation, the micronation could introduce a citizenship rewards system. Citizens who participate in community events, volunteer their time, or contribute to national projects could earn symbolic rewards, such as special citizenship titles, recognition at national events, or access to exclusive resources.

Financial Sustainability: How to Keep the Micronation Running

Financial sustainability is a common challenge for micronations. To ensure its long-term viability, the Cebumicronation would need to establish a steady stream of income while keeping costs manageable.

Tourism Revenue

As mentioned earlier, tourism could be a key source of income for the micronation. By promoting cultural tours, ecotourism, and special events, the micronation could attract visitors from around the world and generate revenue through ticket sales, merchandise, and services.

Symbolic Taxes and Contributions

Citizens could be asked to contribute to the micronation's budget through symbolic taxes or donations. These contributions could be voluntary, with citizens choosing how much they wish to give in support of national projects. In return, citizens could receive special titles or recognition for their contributions.

Partnerships and Grants

The micronation could seek partnerships with local businesses, international organizations, and cultural institutions. These partnerships could provide funding or resources for specific projects, such as environmental conservation efforts or cultural preservation programs.

Potential Conflicts with Local or National Authorities

While the micronation is a symbolic project, it must carefully navigate its relationships with both local and national governments. To avoid conflicts, the micronation would need to operate within the bounds of Philippine law and maintain a cooperative relationship with the authorities.

Staying Within Legal Limits

The micronation would need to ensure that its activities do not infringe on the Philippines' sovereignty or violate national laws. For example, the micronation could refrain from issuing passports or currency that could be mistaken for legal tender. Instead, these items could be clearly marked as symbolic or ceremonial.

Diplomatic Engagement

By fostering open lines of communication with both local and national officials, the micronation could avoid misunderstandings and build positive relationships. Regular meetings with government representatives could help address any concerns and ensure that the micronation is viewed as a positive cultural initiative.

Learning from Micronations: Successes and Failures

There is much to learn from the successes and failures of other micronations around the world. By studying their experiences, Cebu's micronation could avoid common pitfalls and implement best practices that lead to long-term success.

Studying Successful Micronations

Micronations like Sealand and Liberland have gained international attention and built strong communities of supporters. Cebu's micronation could learn from their efforts in branding, diplomacy, and community engagement.

Avoiding Common Pitfalls

Some micronations have struggled with internal conflicts, lack of engagement, or financial difficulties. By learning from these experiences, Cebu's micronation could implement strategies to prevent similar issues from arising.

Continuous Improvement

The micronation could adopt a policy of continuous improvement, regularly evaluating its programs, governance, and initiatives to ensure they meet the needs of its citizens and align with its goals.

CHAPTER 15

THE FUTURE OF THE CEBU MICRONATION

Expanding the Micronation's Global Presence

As the Cebu micronation grows, it could seek to expand its global presence through increased engagement with international organizations, the micronation community, and global movements for cultural preservation and sustainability.

International Outreach

The micronation could develop an international outreach program, engaging with cultural organizations, environmental groups, and international NGOs. These partnerships could help the micronation gain visibility and access to resources that support its mission.

Participation in Global Movements

By aligning itself with global movements for climate action, heritage preservation, and sustainable development, the micronation could become a leader in these areas. This could attract support from international stakeholders and increase the micronation's influence on the world stage.

Building the Cebu Micronation's Legacy

The long-term success of the micronation would depend on its ability to leave a lasting legacy of cultural preservation, sustainability, and innovation. The leadership would need to focus on building institutions and programs that continue to thrive for generations.

Cultural Legacy

The micronation could focus on preserving Cebuano traditions, language, and arts through its educational programs, museums, and cultural festivals. By documenting and sharing these cultural treasures, the micronation could ensure that future generations continue to value and uphold Cebuano heritage.

Environmental Legacy

The micronation's commitment to environmental sustainability could leave a lasting impact on Cebu's ecosystems and natural resources. Through its conservation programs, renewable energy projects, and sustainable agriculture initiatives, the micronation could protect Cebu's natural beauty for generations to come.

Continuing to Innovate: How to Adapt to Circumstances

To remain relevant and successful, the micronation would need to continually adapt to changing circumstances, whether they involve shifts in global politics, technology, or environmental challenges.

Technological Innovation

As new technologies emerge, the micronation could integrate them into its governance, economy, and education systems. This could include expanding its digital infrastructure, adopting new renewable energy sources, or using data analytics to improve urban planning and resource management.

Responsive Governance

The micronation's leadership would need to remain responsive to the needs of its citizens, ensuring that policies and programs evolve in line with the changing priorities of the community. Regular consultations with citizens, continuous feedback loops, and updates to the micronation's constitution would help maintain an adaptive and responsive governance system.

Environmental Resilience

As climate change and environmental issues continue to escalate, the micronation could invest in resilience-building strategies to protect its natural resources and infrastructure. This could include expanding reforestation projects, improving coastal protection measures, and investing in disaster preparedness.

Maintaining Cultural Relevance in a Globalized World

In an increasingly globalized world, where cultures blend and change at a rapid pace, maintaining Cebu's distinct cultural identity would be a key challenge. The micronation would need to balance tradition with modernity, ensuring that it remains culturally relevant while preserving its unique heritage.

Embracing Modern Interpretations of Culture

While the micronation would focus on preserving traditional Cebuano practices, it could also encourage modern interpretations of these traditions. By supporting contemporary Cebuano artists, musicians, and filmmakers who draw on their cultural roots, the micronation could ensure that its culture remains dynamic and continues to evolve with the times.

Cultural Diplomacy

Engaging in cultural diplomacy could help promote Cebu's heritage on a global scale. By sending cultural ambassadors to international festivals, hosting cultural exchange programs, and participating in global cultural forums, the micronation could foster greater appreciation and understanding of Cebuano culture worldwide.

Digital Presence

To stay relevant, the micronation could expand its digital presence, using social media, online exhibitions, and virtual reality experiences to share Cebu's culture with a global audience. By harnessing the power of technology, the micronation could make its cultural initiatives accessible to people far beyond its physical borders.

The Cebu Micronation's Role in Global Movements for Autonomy, Independence, and Self-Determination

As a symbolic project, the Cebumicronation could play a role in global discussions around autonomy, cultural preservation, and self-determination. By aligning itself with these movements, the micronation could gain visibility and contribute to important conversations about the rights of regions and peoples to assert their identities.

Advocating for Cultural Autonomy

The micronation could become a leading voice in advocating for cultural autonomy, both within the Philippines and on the global stage. By promoting the idea that regions have the right to preserve their unique heritage while remaining part of larger political structures, the micronation could inspire similar projects around the world.

Engaging with Indigenous and Minority Movements

The micronation could also engage with indigenous peoples and minority groups who are fighting for their own cultural preservation and self-determination. By building alliances and sharing best practices, the micronation could help support global efforts to protect endangered cultures and languages.

A Model for Sustainable Governance

Finally, the Cebu micronation could serve as a model for sustainable governance, demonstrating how a small community can balance environmental stewardship, cultural preservation, and modern governance. By showcasing its success in these areas, the micronation could influence other regions and communities seeking to create more sustainable and culturally focused forms of governance.

CHAPTER 16

MAKING THE CEBU MICRONATION DREAM A REALITY

Creating a micronation is no small feat, but with the right vision, dedication, and community engagement, the dream of a Cebu micronation can become a reality.

Throughout this book, we have explored the many facets of building a symbolic nation, from governance structures and cultural preservation to sustainability and diplomacy.

The Cebu micronation would be more than just a political project—it would be a celebration of Cebuano identity, a beacon for sustainability, and a symbol of how regions can assert their cultural autonomy in a respectful and cooperative manner.

By focusing on culture, community, and innovation, the micronation could inspire not just the people of Cebu but others around the world who are passionate about preserving their heritage and creating a brighter, more sustainable future.

Recapping the Key Steps to Micronation Creation

Define the Vision and Purpose

Decide on the goals of the micronation, whether it's cultural preservation, sustainability, or promoting local governance.

Establish Legal and Political Frameworks

Draft a constitution, create a system of governance, and establish laws that reflect the micronation's values.

Develop Cultural and Environmental Initiatives

Focus on preserving Cebuano culture through education, festivals, and the arts, while promoting sustainability and environmental protection.

Engage Citizens and Build Community

Foster a sense of national identity through active citizenship, community events, and rewards for participation.

Create Diplomatic and Global Alliances

Build relationships with other micronations, cultural organizations, and international movements that align with the micronation's goals.

Inspiring a New Generation of Cebuano Leaders Citizens

One of the most important outcomes of the Cebu micronation would be the inspiration it provides to future generations. By instilling a sense of pride in their Cebuano identity and teaching the values of sustainability, cultural preservation, and community engagement, the micronation could help shape the next generation of leaders and citizens.

Young people could play a central role in the micronation's growth, bringing fresh ideas and energy to its projects. The micronation would ensure its legacy by empowering youth to participate in governance, education, and innovation.

The Symbolic Importance of Micronations in the Century

In the 21st century, micronations have taken on new significance as symbolic expressions of autonomy, identity, and innovation. While they may not be recognized as sovereign states, they serve as important platforms for communities to explore new forms of governance, cultural preservation, and sustainability.

The Cebu micronation would stand as a testament to the power of cultural identity, showing that even in an interconnected and globalized world, regions can assert their unique heritage and values. By creating an atmosphere of pride and responsibility among its citizens, the micronation could contribute to the global conversation about autonomy, self-determination, and sustainable governance.

The creation of a Cebu micronation would be a bold and exciting project—one that honors the past, addresses the challenges of the present, and builds a brighter, more sustainable future for all. Through community, culture, and innovation, Cebu could become a model for how regions and people can reclaim their identity and create a thriving, symbolic nation.

Chapter 17

Appendices

Appendix 1: Draft Constitution of the Republic of Cebu

Preamble:

We, the people of Cebu, united in our shared heritage and commitment to preserving our culture, environment, and community, hereby establish this micronation to promote the values of sustainability, cultural pride, and responsible governance. We pledge to uphold the principles of democracy, peace, and cooperation, ensuring that our nation thrives for future generations.

Article I: National Sovereignty and Cultural Identity

1. The Republic of Cebu is a symbolic micronation committed to preserving Cebuano heritage and promoting environmental sustainability.

2. The micronation does not seek political independence

but operates as a cultural and symbolic entity within the framework of the Philippines.

Article II: Government and Structure

1. The micronation shall be governed by a president, elected by the citizens every four years, and a Council of Elders, which shall advise the government on matters of culture and tradition.

2. The legislative body, the Cebuano Assembly, shall be composed of representatives from various regions and sectors, who will enact laws in accordance with the micronation's constitution.

Article III: Citizenship

1. Citizenship is open to all who pledge allegiance to the values and mission of the micronation, with special consideration given to those of Cebuano heritage.

2. Citizens are entitled to participate in elections, referendums, and cultural programs and have the duty to contribute to the micronation's sustainability and cultural preservation initiatives.

Article IV: Environmental Stewardship

1. The Republic of Cebu shall prioritize environmental sustainability in all its endeavors, with special protections for marine life, forests, and natural resources.

2. Citizens and businesses are required to adhere to environmentally friendly practices, including recycling, conservation, and the use of renewable energy.

Article V: Preservation

1. The Republic of Cebu is dedicated to the preservation of Cebuano language, traditions, and arts.

2. National festivals, education programs, and museums shall be established to promote and protect Cebuano culture.

Article VI: Relations

1. The Republic of Cebu shall engage in peaceful and cooperative diplomacy with other micronations and cultural organizations.

2. The Republic of Cebu shall actively pursue international partnerships that align with the values of sustainability and cultural preservation.

Sample National Symbols (Flag, Anthem, Currency)

1. Flag: A blue and green flag, symbolizing the sea and land, with a central emblem of Magellan's Cross surrounded by traditional Cebuano patterns.

2. Anthem: "Sa Kahayag sa Kalinaw" (In the Light of Peace), a song that reflects Cebu's peaceful history and commitment to unity and cultural pride.

3. Currency: Cebuano pesos, with denominations featuring images of Lapu-Lapu, the Basilica del Santo Niño, and the Sinulog Festival.

Appendix 2: Useful Resources for Micronation Creators

1. United Micronations Multi-Oceanic Archipelago: A forum where micronations can discuss their projects, share ideas, and form alliances.

2. International Micronation Summit: An annual event where micronation leaders gather to share their experiences and collaborate on global initiatives.

3. Cultural Heritage Organizations: UNESCO, the International Council on Monuments and Sites (ICOMOS), and other organizations that can provide support for cultural preservation efforts.

Appendix 3: Glossary of Terms

1. Micronation: A self-declared, symbolic nation that is not recognized as a sovereign state by established governments or international organizations.

2. Sustainability: Practices that ensure the preservation and responsible management of natural resources for future generations.

3. Cultural Preservation: The protection, celebration, and transmission of a group's cultural heritage, in-

cluding language, traditions, and arts.

4. Symbolic Governance: A form of governance that, while not legally recognized, represents the will and values of a community in a non-political, often cultural or ceremonial, way.

5. Autonomy: The ability of a region or community to govern itself independently, though not necessarily seeking full political sovereignty.

Acknowledgements

This book is a product of collective imagination, creativity, and love for Cebu's rich history and culture. I would like to express my deep gratitude to the scholars, cultural historians, environmentalists, and local leaders of Cebu who have dedicated their time to preserving and promoting Cebuano heritage. Without their efforts, this micronation project could not be envisioned.

Special thanks to the global micronation community for their creativity and vision, which has inspired this work and served as a model for what can be achieved when people come together with a shared dream.

Lastly, I would like to thank the readers who will take this concept and continue to explore what is possible. Whether you are a Cebuano proud of your heritage, a creative visionary, or a global citizen interested in the future of cultural preservation, this journey has only just begun.

Final Thoguhts

Thank you for embarking on this journey of imagination, cultural pride, and innovation. The dream of a Cebu micronation is both a tribute to the rich history of the island and a call to action for future generations to cherish and protect their heritage. Whether as a symbolic nation or a creative project, the Republic of Cebu offers a vision of what is possible when a community comes together with a shared goal of sustainability, cultural preservation, and unity. The future is bright, and it starts now—within each of us who believe in the power of identity, tradition, and progress.

ABOUT THE AUTHOR

Prof. Basilio Ojas, PhD, is a cultural historian and advocate for sustainability and local autonomy. With a deep passion for Cebuano culture, Prof. Basilio Ojas, PhD, has dedicated his career to researching and promoting the unique heritage of the Visayas region. As a writer, educator, and environmentalist, he has worked with local communities to preserve traditional practices and explore innovative solutions for sustainable development.

Prof. Basilio Ojas, PhD, is also an active participant in the global micronation community and has spoken at various international forums on the importance of cultural preservation in the modern world. This book is a culmination of years of research, creative exploration, and advocacy for a more sustainable and culturally vibrant future for Cebu and beyond.